Granddaddy's Gift

MARGAREE KING MITCHELL

Granddaddy's Gift

ILLUSTRATED BY LARRY JOHNSON

BridgeWater Paperback

Granddaddy's name was Joe Morgan. I followed my
Granddaddy everywhere, so people called me Little Joe.
But Granddaddy called me Daughter.

I grew up on a farm in Mississippi with Grandmama and Granddaddy. Most people at the time didn't have much. Granddaddy owned his own land. He raised cows, pigs, and horses. He grew cotton, corn, and cucumbers. Grandmama had a garden, and we always had tomatoes, butter beans, and black-eyed peas.

Granddaddy had only gotten as far as the eighth grade. He would have had to leave home to go further, and his daddy didn't have the money to send him. So he worked in the fields, saved his money, and bought his land a little at a time. He ordered books through the mail and read them by the light of the fireplace.

One particular morning, when I was eight years old, I slowed around until the big yellow school bus left without me. I didn't want to go to school anymore.

It had rained for several days, and this was the first time it was dry enough for Granddaddy to plow the fields. Well, he must have had X-ray eyes, because as soon as the bus pulled away, he stopped the tractor and came into the house. "Daughter, get your books together," he said.

We got in the black truck and rode the thirty miles to school. On the way we rode past a cotton field full of workers, some of them my age.

I asked why I had to go to school. I already knew how to read and write, and the books we had at home were better than the books at school. Those books, passed down from the white schools, were raggedy, with pages missing.

"Daughter," Granddaddy said sadly, "I know they're not teaching you everything they should, but you have to go to school. I want you to learn as much as you can so when you grow up, you can choose what you want to do. I didn't have that choice."

That night after supper Granddaddy said he was taking us to a meeting. We all got in the truck, me, my brother, and sisters. Granddaddy turned off onto a dirt road and drove for a long time.

He told us that many years ago, segregation laws had been passed in the South to keep black people from having the same rights as white people, like the right to vote. He said it was important to vote, that it was a way for our voices to be heard.

When we finally arrived at a church, the parking lot was full and cars were lined up on both sides of the road. We found a place to stand in the back of the church. A lawyer, Mr. James Marshall, was asking for volunteers. He wanted someone to try to register to vote.

At first nobody said anything. Then, from the back of the room, Granddaddy raised his hand. "I'll go," he said.

The meeting ended with a song and a prayer for Granddaddy. In those days it was dangerous for people to stand up for their rights.

The next day Granddaddy rode into town and parked his truck in front of the courthouse. He walked like he was going some-where, the way he always did. As usual, I was right behind him.

He went into one of the offices and told the lady behind the counter that he wanted to register to vote.

The lady went into the back room and came back with a man. "Well, now, Joe," the man said. "You see, there is this test you have to take on the Mississippi Constitution. It's hard, real hard. You're doing all right, Joe. Just be satisfied with what you have."

Granddaddy left the office. I turned and walked after him, my head hanging down. I didn't want to look at Granddaddy's face, because I knew he felt bad, too.

He waited for me at the top of the courthouse steps. He took my hand. "Daughter," he said, "hold your head up high. We have done nothing wrong."

Granddaddy told me there was something important to strive for in addition to the good things we had. There were some things that made a person feel good inside, like having the rights we were all entitled to as citizens of these United States.

I didn't understand everything then, but I lifted my head. The sun was shining.

We started going by Mr. Marshall's house whenever we went to town. Mr. Marshall would go over the constitution with Granddaddy and ask him questions. I was supposed to be doing my homework, but I was listening, too. I answered the questions right along with Granddaddy.

On the day that Granddaddy went to the courthouse with Mr. Marshall to take the test, a big crowd gathered outside. People started shouting and calling Granddaddy bad names. Granddaddy had on his Sunday suit. Somebody pulled the coat and tore it.

The police met Granddaddy and
Mr. Marshall at the door of the courthouse.
They asked Granddaddy why he was trying
to cause trouble. He told them he was just
trying to register to vote.

In the back room of the courthouse, he
answered all twenty-two questions.
Granddaddy passed the test. But he and
Mr. Marshall had to leave through the
back door of the courthouse.

The news spread quickly that Granddaddy was now a
registered voter. That night we all got in the truck and headed
to the church. There was going to be a big celebration. As we
drove up, we could see bright orange flames shooting up
against the dark sky.

After the church burned down, people's fear turned into determination, and more men and women came forward to register to vote.

I understood why Granddaddy had wanted me to go to school. I never skipped school again, even if we did have raggedy books.

On my eighteenth birthday, when I went to register to vote, Granddaddy came with me. I didn't have to take a test on the constitution. I just had to fill out a card with my name, address, and date of birth. Now I could vote and make my own voice heard.

Granddaddy had taught me to stand up for things, even if I was scared, and always to be proud. His gift never left me.

At the top of the courthouse steps, Granddaddy took my hand. We had come a long way. We still had a long way to go.

To Ben, Cynthia, Ira, Camilla,
Vidalia, Johnnie, Jean, Ronnie,
recipients of the Gift. —M.K.M.

I thank God for allowing us the
opportunity to become grandparents.
It's always easier to find the right
place the second time around. —L.J.

Text copyright © 1997 by Margaree King Mitchell.
Illustrations copyright © 1997 by Larry Johnson.

Published by BridgeWater Paperback, an imprint and
trademark of Troll Communications L.L.C.

First published in hardcover by BridgeWater Books.

First paperback edition published 1998.

Printed in the United States of America.
Book design by Sylvia Frezzolini Severance.
Edited by Pamela D. Pollack.

10 9 8 7 6 5 4 3 2 1

Library of Congress Cataloging-in-Publication Data

Mitchell, Margaree King.
    Granddaddy's gift / by Margaree King Mitchell;
pictures by Larry Johnson.
        p.   cm.
        Summary: When her grandfather registers to vote while living
in segregated Mississippi, an Afro-American girl begins to understand
why he insists that she attend school.
        ISBN 0-8167-4010-0 (lib. bdg.)   ISBN 0-8167-4011-9 (pbk.)
        1. Afro-Americans—Mississippi—Juvenile fiction.
[1. Afro-Americans—Mississippi—Fiction.
2. Mississippi—Fiction. 3. Grandfathers—Fiction.
4. Voting—Fiction.] I. Johnson, Larry, 1949- ill.
II. Title.
    PZ7.M6937Gr 1997
    [E]—dc20   95-41102